For Grace M.P.
For Charlie T.H.

First published in Great Britain in 1998 by Ragged Bears Limited,
Ragged Appleshaw, Andover, Hampshire SP11 9HX

Text copyright © 1998 by Mal Peet
Illustration copyright © 1998 by Tudor Humphries

Cover design by Janet McCallum

*A CIP record of this book
is available from the British Library*

ISBN 1 85714 147 4

Printed in Hong Kong

A Floating World

Mal Peet &
Tudor Humphries

Ragged Bears

It floated beautifully, the boat, just like Grandad said it would. It didn't tip or wobble as it drifted out into the middle of the garden pond, to where Neil couldn't quite reach it.

The rain came very suddenly, and it wasn't gentle.
It was a hard, stinging rain like little bits of glass
thrown in your face. The sky turned the colour of a
bruise, and Neil ran. He left the boat where it was.

The rain beat at the windows for the rest of that
day, and all through the night, and all through the
next day and all through the next night.

On the third day of the Great Rain, Neil saw that all the puddles in the garden were joining up into one huge puddle. He went out to rescue the boat. It had floated to the edge of the pond and Neil bent down to lift it out of the water. Then he saw the spiders. One was already on the boat. The other was lowering itself on a thread from a branch of the tree which grew beside the pond. Neil reached up and very carefully took the spider in his hand.

Its legs tickled inside his gentle fist.
He put it safely on board the boat.

Neil stood up to think. All around him the world was turning to water. Rain spattered into puddles, water gurgled in drainpipes, gargled in gutters. Thick brown water from the fields slipped through the hedge into the garden.

The word FLOOD floated into Neil's head.

First, he splodged over to the compost heap. There he found a worm, a big one, washed pink. It bulged and twisted on the wet palm of Neil's hand. With his other hand, he carefully dug into the warm dark mess of the compost heap until he found a second plump pink worm. He carried them and a handful of compost over to the boat and put them in.

When he lifted the brick, the woodlice ran about in daft circles as if the sudden light had made them blind. There were two sorts; the ones that curled up into a tight little ball, and the ones that didn't. The ones that curled up were called pill bugs. His Mum had told him that long ago people used to swallow them as medicine. The thought made him feel slightly sick. Imagine curling yourself up for safety and then being picked up by giant fingers and being swallowed alive ...

The two pill bugs rolled around in his hands. The other two tried to escape through his fingers. Neil felt twenty-eight tiny pale legs exploring his skin. He put all four woodlice into the boat.

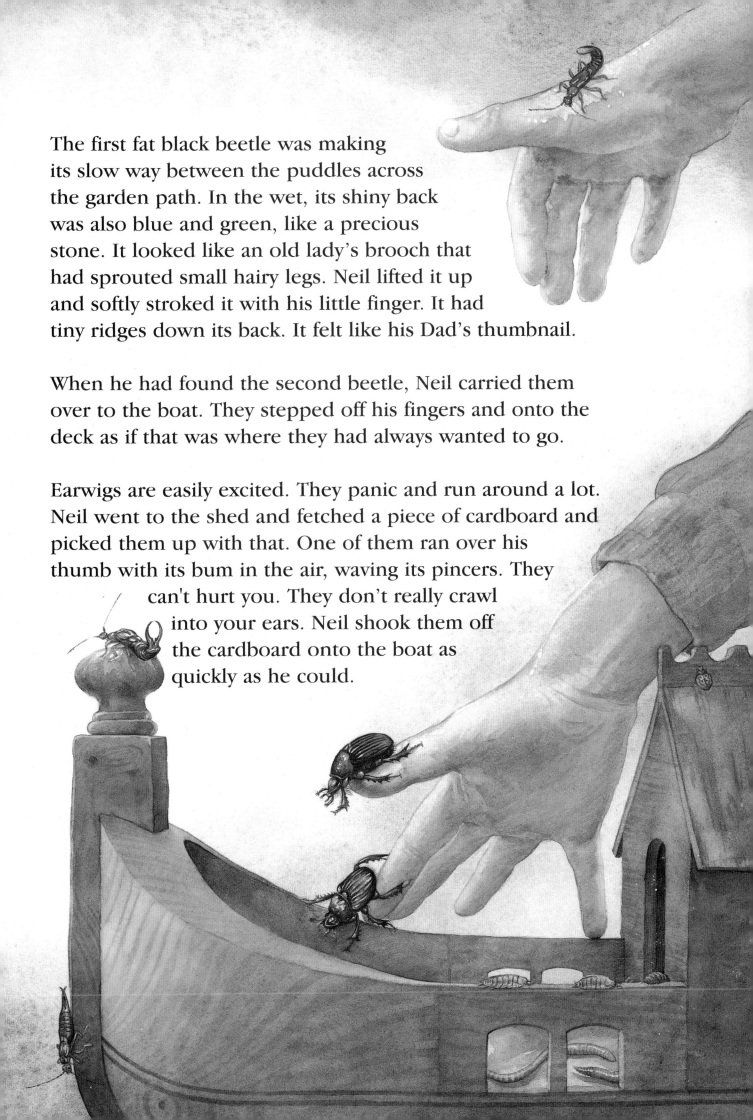

The first fat black beetle was making
its slow way between the puddles across
the garden path. In the wet, its shiny back
was also blue and green, like a precious
stone. It looked like an old lady's brooch that
had sprouted small hairy legs. Neil lifted it up
and softly stroked it with his little finger. It had
tiny ridges down its back. It felt like his Dad's thumbnail.

When he had found the second beetle, Neil carried them
over to the boat. They stepped off his fingers and onto the
deck as if that was where they had always wanted to go.

Earwigs are easily excited. They panic and run around a lot.
Neil went to the shed and fetched a piece of cardboard and
picked them up with that. One of them ran over his
thumb with its bum in the air, waving its pincers. They
can't hurt you. They don't really crawl
into your ears. Neil shook them off
the cardboard onto the boat as
quickly as he could.

Ladybirds eat blackfly.

Find blackfly, and you'll find ladybirds.

The runner beans grew up a kind of wigwam of bamboo poles at the edge of the vegetable garden. The vegetable garden was slowly disappearing under the puddles that lay everywhere like broken mirrors. Neil's boots went through the bright water into the deep squelch of mud beneath. He lifted a sprig of bean leaves and the blackfly were there, lumps of them on the stems of the plants. The ladybirds were there too, sitting under their green umbrellas, waiting to feel hungry again.

What Neil liked about ladybirds,
as well as their scarlet and
black-spotted circus jackets, was
that they always seemed quite
happy to walk about on your hands.
Sometimes you'd have to blow on them to
get them to open their jackets, get their
wings out and fly away. But today, just to
make sure, Neil carried them to the boat
inside cupped hands and put them in,
along with a sprig of bean leaves thickly
coated with blackfly.

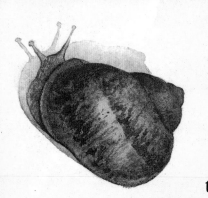

Next, snails. It was a perfect snaily day, and they were out enjoying it, slithering their bellies along the wet ground beside the drain outside the kitchen. The wall there was silvery with snail-trails. Neil liked snails. He liked the whirlpool pattern of their shells, and he liked the way their eyes grew on stalks. If you very gently touched those eyestalks, it was amazing how fast they'd disappear. He crouched down over one of his snails and put the tip of his finger against the eyestalks.

Gone.

He turned the snail upside down and watched its gluey foot tuck itself up into the shell. He carried a pair of snails down through the rain to the boat. The rain was heavier now, and the edge of the sky was turning dark. He heard his mother calling him, telling him tea was ready, telling him to be sure to wash his hands. Neil stood, feeling cold looking at the boat and the dark little movements inside it. He knew what he had to do, and he didn't want to do it.

The slugs were the thick wrinkly ones, the colour of an orange gone rotten. The cardboard he'd used for the earwigs was useless now; it was soggy and falling to pieces. He tried using a stick, but as soon as he touched one of the slugs it did a horrible sort of twitch and rolled over. In the end he picked it up without looking at it. The he picked up another one. They squirmed in his hand like a pair of slimy lips. It was like being kissed by the Bogeyman. He ran down to the pond, tasting the sick in his throat, and threw them onto the boat. He hoped he hadn't hurt them.

At tea-time, he didn't fancy the rice pudding.

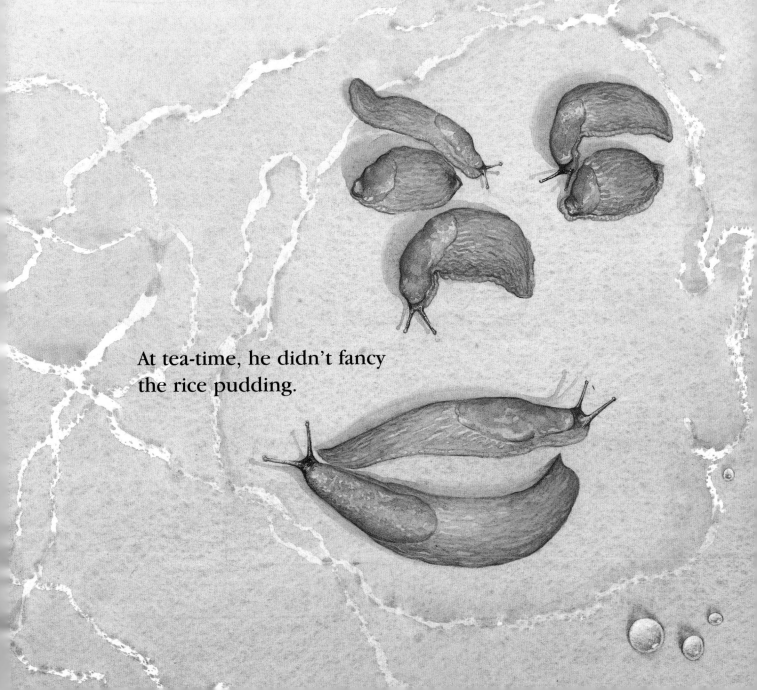

It was around the middle of the next day that the rain slowed and then stopped. Neil opened his bedroom window and looked out at a world of water. His house was a ship, a ship drifting on an enormous lake. The garden path, the pond and the hedge were all gone, and the fields beyond were one glimmering sheet of water. Here and there the tops of the tallest trees grew out of their own reflections. A mile away, the wood on the hill humped in the water like a great blue whale.

Above it all, the clouds sat in the sky like huge heaps of wet grey washing. There was no boat.

At tea-time, the great bundles of cloud grew fatter and heavier and then the rain began again.

The rain fell for three more days and nights. Sometimes it fell hard, straight down from the sky like pebbles. Sometimes it was soft as fog.

But it never stopped altogether.

Neil watched the flood creep up from the garden
and across the patio almost as far as the kitchen door.
Maybe he should have been worried, maybe even scared.
But he was too bored.

He was bored to death. Each wet grey hour
seemed to last a week. The flood made him a
prisoner in his own house.

Neil was the kind of boy who liked to come awake slowly, like a bubble rising to the surface of a pond. So when he woke up on the eighth morning of the flood, it took him a little while to realise that the world had changed during the night. Brilliant light rainbowed his room. He listened for the drumming of the rain, but what he heard instead was a bird singing. He yanked the curtains apart and shoved the window open. He was dazzled by sunlight and had to screw up his eyes. When he could open them he looked up at the sky where the wind was chasing and tearing the clouds, leaving huge spaces of blue.

The water that surrounded the house flashed and
glittered in the sunlight.

All through the rest of that day, the flood slid back down
the garden, inch by inch. It left a raggedy line of rubbish
and twigs along the edge of the patio. The trees grew
taller in the water.

Neil went to bed late that night. From his window he saw a world of silver and black beneath the moon. And he thought he saw a black shape slide out of the shadow of a tree.

It may have been the next day, or the day after, that
a gleaming black beetle struggled up onto the roof
of the boat. It felt the air with its small whiskery face.
It walked carefully to the far end of the roof and stopped.
It stood quite still for a second or two, then its shell lifted
and separated. Wings appeared, and suddenly the beetle
was in the air, a blur of dangly legs. It flew in all
directions until all its strength was gone, but the world
was still all water. There was nowhere to land, and the
beetle clattered back to the boat and crept into the
darkness inside.

It was a day later that a ladybird climbed onto the roof. It turned one way, and then another, feeling for the breeze. Then its scarlet jacket opened, wings sprouted, and the ladybird was off, into the air.

The ladybird didn't come back.

After a wild

and zig-zag flight,

it found something dry,

and soft,

and green

to land on.

Neil bent down and lifted the ark out of the great puddle that was all that was left of the Great Flood. He did it slowly, so that he wouldn't disturb the ladybird resting on his hat. He put the ark up on the small mountain of the compost heap and opened the door in the side of the boat. And one by one, and two by two, Neil's animals slithered and scuttled and crept out into their world again.